The River

Illustrated by Hanako Clulow

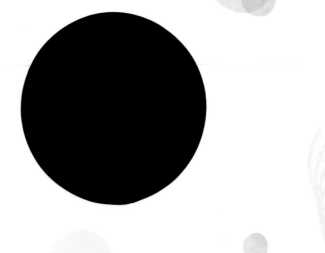

In snow-capped mountains, among the firs,

The north wind blows; something stirs.

This is where she's meant to be!

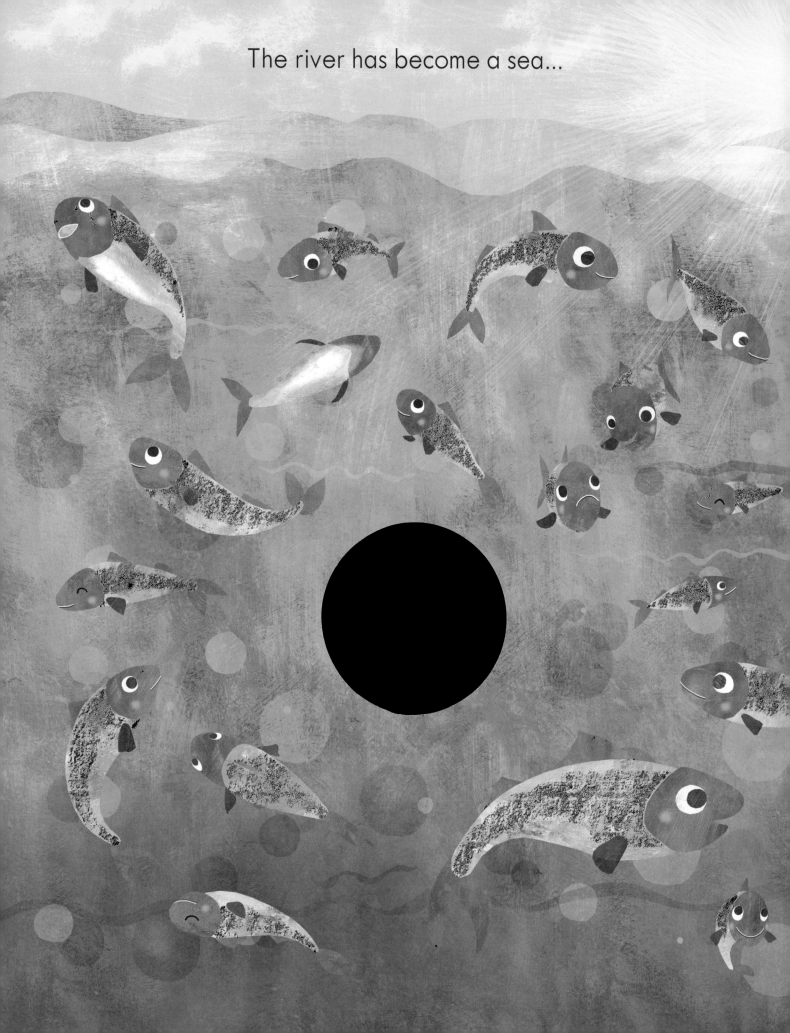

The river has become a sea...

The fish swims on and on, until...

The days grow longer, the air is still.

Through snow and wind and rain and sun,

The fish must finish what she's begun.

On the riverbank, two bear cubs play,
And so begins a brand new day.

The moon shines down, the whole world sleeps.

Below, the little fish dives and leaps.

An owl hoots softly, branches sway.

The fish continues on her way.

Busy beavers scamper and scurry.

The fish swims on — hurry, hurry!

Faster, faster, the wide river flows,
Rushing, gushing, then it slows.

A deer looks up and sniffs the air,

The fish travels on to who knows where?

Through pine forests, still as night,

The water glints in dappled light.

Down the mountain, through ice floes,

On and on, the little fish goes.

The river sparkles under a sunlit sky.
Overhead, white snow geese fly.

Through icy water, a small fish darts —
This is where her journey starts...